Suzy Kline
Mary Marony
Hides Out

Illustrations by Blanche Sims

A YEARLING BOOK

To my editor,

Anne O'Connell

*With appreciation for your hard work,
insight, questions and,* especially,
your love of the characters.

Published by
Bantam Doubleday Dell Books for Young Readers
a division of
Bantam Doubleday Dell Publishing Group, Inc.
1540 Broadway
New York, New York 10036

Acknowledgments

Special thanks to . . .

Rufus, who thought of the title.

Mom, who read the first draft.

Speech therapists Dot Barlow and

Ann Dillon for their consultation.

The students at my author lunches for their inspiration.

And my second graders for their comments.

Text copyright © 1993 by Suzy Kline
Illustrations copyright © 1993 by Blanche Sims

ISBN: 0-440-41135-1

Reprinted by arrangement with G. P. Putnam's Sons, a division of The Putnam & Grosset Group

Printed in the United States of America

March 1996

10 9 8 7 6 5 4 3 2 1

CWO

Contents

1

The Author Is Coming!

Mary Marony tapped her feet while she hugged her new book, *Ghost in the Clock*. She was so excited! Today she was meeting her favorite author, Jan Berry.

Marvin Higgins, who was supposed to be sharpening his pencil, took a quick peek around the door. "THEY'RE LINING UP!" he shouted.

Mrs. Bird pointed to Marvin's seat.

"Sit down, Marvin."

As soon as Marvin sat down, she said, "Line up!"

Mary quickly stood behind her friends, Audrey Tang and Elizabeth Conway.

"I can't wait," Elizabeth said.

"Muh-muh-me too," Mary stuttered. Then the three girls jumped up and down, giggling and squealing.

Mrs. Bird shot the girls a look. "Shhh! Shhh!" she snapped.

Mary thought she *looked* like a bird pecking at something.

"Shhh! Shhh!"

Finally, when everyone was quiet, the teacher turned and led the class down the hall.

"You have Jan Berry's newest book!" Audrey whispered. "Gee, it's not even in our school library yet."

Mary beamed. "Dad got it for muh-
me last Saturday at the bookstore. I
can't w-wait to get it autographed."

When other children started talking,
Mrs. Bird turned around and pointed to
the principal's office.

"Shhhh! Shhhh!
We're walking in the hall
Someone in the office
Might be making a call!"

The class smiled. They loved it when Mrs. Bird said poems. Quickly they repeated this new one, moving their heads from side to side as they kept the beat.

"Shhhh! Shhhh!
We're walking in the hall
Someone in the office
Might be making a call!"

Now Mrs. Bird smiled. Her class was standing tall with hands to their sides, lips closed, heads high, and eyes on her. Proudly, she turned and marched them to the auditorium.

The principal was pleased to greet them at the door. *"Good morning,* boys and girls!"

"Good morning, Mr. Fries," everyone replied.

Except Fred Heinz. He whispered, " 'Mornin', French Fries."

Marvin laughed. He liked Fred's jokes.

One by one the classes filled up the auditorium. The second graders got to sit in front because they were the youngest class invited. The sixth graders sat in the back. By the time the third, fourth and fifth graders were seated in the middle rows, the auditorium was *very* noisy.

Mr. Fries walked across the stage carrying a large box. After he set it down, he pulled out something. It was a foghorn. Mary watched him bring the huge instrument up to his lips and blow.

"BERrrrrrrr!"

Students everywhere jumped out of their seats!

When they landed, they were pin quiet.

"I got this foghorn up in Maine last weekend so I could get my secretary's attention."

The teachers groaned.

"But I thought it might come in handy today too. This is an exciting moment for Elm School. We've never had an author visit before. How many of you have read *The Cat Who Liked Iced Tea* or *Cat on Vacation*?"

Mary joined the sea of hands.

"All right!" the principal replied. "Now, the famous author of these books, Jan Berry, will be here for a day and a half, thanks to our Elm School PTA and their spaghetti dinner fund-raiser!"

Everyone applauded politely for the PTA.

"Let's welcome JAN BERRY." And he blew on his foghorn one more time.

2

Muh-muh-mary

"BERrrrrrr!"

Everyone jumped to their feet and clapped. Some students waved signs and posters. Mary kept her eyes on the split between the curtains. She couldn't wait to see what Jan Berry looked like.

Suddenly the author appeared.

Laughing.

Waving.

And holding a basket.

Mary and her friends whispered . . .

"She's s-so tall!"

"Her hair's a mess!"

"She's wearing men's shoes!"

The girls watched the woman in the long denim shirt and wrinkled blouse come to the edge of the stage with a microphone. "It's so nice to be here at Elm School."

Everyone cheered.

"How many of you like to write?"

Mary joined the many children who raised their hands.

"That's wonderful! You know, boys and girls, when I was your age I liked to write too." Then she took some things out of her basket.

"This is the diary I used when I was in third grade, and here are the letters I got from my grandfather. We wrote to each other once a week."

After Jan Berry continued talking about her writing experiences, she asked, "Have any of you read my newest book, *Ghost in the Clock*?"

The audience was quiet.

Audrey nudged Mary. "Raise your hand. You've got it on your lap!"

Mary started to sink down in her seat. No one else was raising his hand. It was too risky. She might have to talk in front of the whole school.

"Go on, Mary!" Elizabeth nudged.

Mary quickly thought about it. All she had to do was raise her hand. She'd done it twice before. Why not a third time?

Slowly, Mary raised her hand.

Jan Berry smiled when she spotted Mary in the second row. "Please stand up so I can see you better."

Mary's heart thumped and her legs wobbled. Audrey and Elizabeth had to help her stand up.

There.

She did it!

"What's your name?" the author asked.

Oh, no! Mary thought. She wasn't supposed to say anything. And now she had to say two *M* words. *M* words were the hardest for her to say!

Marvin whispered behind her, "Go ahead, Muh-muh-mary Muh-muh-marony."

Mary bit her lip. She didn't care about Marvin. She could ignore him. But she couldn't ignore the sea of eyes staring at her. Mary panicked. What did her speech therapist, Miss Lawton, tell her to do? Why couldn't she remember?

Mary tried to speak. "Muh-muh-muh-muh-muh-muh . . ."

Marvin and Fred giggled.

"muh-muh-muh-muh . . ."

"MARY MARONY," Mrs. Bird shouted.

Mary plopped in her seat. HOW EMBARRASSING! Now everyone at Elm School knew she stuttered.

"Thank you, Mary Marony," the author replied. "I'm flattered you have my book. It just arrived in the bookstores."

Mary tried to smile and nod, but the tears kept coming down her cheeks. Quickly, she wiped them away with the sleeves of her blouse, and then the bottom of her skirt.

Elizabeth reached in her pocket and handed Mary a Kleenex. "You were

very brave."

"I w-was d-dumb!" Mary groaned. Now she was stuttering on every word.

Audrey turned around and sneered. "I'm telling on you, Marvin Higgins."

"D-don't! J-just f-forget it," Mary replied. She didn't care about Marvin. She cared about the author. How could she ever talk to her again? There was no way she was getting an autograph now. Mary wished she could just run and hide somewhere.

3

Mary Marony Hides Out

At lunch recess, Mary ran to the bathroom and hid behind the big yellow
door that had the word GIRLS and a
little skirted figure on the front.

Mary pulled her knees close to her
chest and started rereading her book,
Ghost in the Clock. When she got to
page twelve, Audrey and Elizabeth ran
in.

"THERE YOU ARE!" Elizabeth exclaimed as she peeked around the door.

"Why are you hiding?" Audrey asked.

"You heard muh-me stutter in fr-front of the school."

"So?" the girls replied.

"S-so it was embarrassing. Mrs. Bird even had to f-finish saying my name. I d-don't want anyone to see muh-me for a while."

"Can we hide with you?" Elizabeth asked.

"We can't fit back there," Audrey said, eyeing the mop bucket in the corner.

"Sure we can," Elizabeth replied, wheeling the big silver pail into the janitor's closet. "Come on!"

The girls giggled as they squished together behind the door. As soon as they heard someone come in, they motioned to zip their lips.

Very quietly, the girls listened to the different sounds of the bathroom. The footsteps, stall doors being bolted and unbolted, toilets flushing, water spraying in the sink and the pump, pump, pumping of the soap dispenser.

Now, there was the sound of ripping paper towels, and voices.

"Isn't it neat that Jan Berry is visiting the sixth-grade classes. I can't wait until she comes to our room."

"Me either. What about the author's lunch tomorrow?"

"Only one person gets to go from each class. Our teacher is drawing a name out of a hat. Wish me luck!"

"Wish *me* luck. We have to write an

essay on why we want to have lunch with Jan Berry. Whoever has the best paper goes. That means recopying at *least* twice."

"AAaaaaaugh . . . ," the girls complained as they covered their mouths with their paper towels and pretended to gag.

"Let's get out of here!"

As soon as the bathroom was quiet again, Elizabeth started talking.

"This is so much fun! I love eavesdropping. No one knows we're here!"

"I know *that Lysol smell* from the mop bucket is still here," Audrey said as she twirled the empty spools of thread on her necklace. "And I bet Mrs. Bird forgot about that author lunch tomorrow. She never told us about it."

"Oh, don't be such a worrywart,"

Elizabeth snapped. "You know how Mrs. Bird likes to surprise us. She probably has it all planned."

Audrey shrugged. Someone had just come into the bathroom, and they had to stop talking.

After the girls listened to the footsteps, there were no other sounds. What was going on? they wondered as they huddled behind the door.

A third grader was looking in the mirror, tying a bow around her ponytail. After she stepped back and admired the paw prints on her pink ribbon, she began singing and dancing.

"La ti dah

Dee dah

Dee doo.

John Jacob Finkledinkle

I love you."

The moment she stopped singing, the girls broke out laughing.

"WHO'S IN HERE?" the girl shouted.

Mary covered her mouth.

Elizabeth covered her face.

Audrey hung on to her necklace with both hands.

Suddenly the bathroom door was slammed shut.

BLAM!

"So. . . . *THERE* YOU ARE!" the girl yelled. "THREE SECOND-GRADE SPIES!"

30

Mary stood up. "We . . . we . . . didn't muh-mean to spy. We were r-reading. S-see?" she said, holding up her book. Mary knew that's what she *meant* to do.

"I remember you," the third grader said. "Your class sat in front of us at that author assembly. You're the one who stuttered."

Mary put her head down. She didn't want to talk any more.

"Don't you know it's very *ruh-ruh-rude* to spy?"

Tears rushed to Mary's eyes. She hated it when people made fun of her stuttering. When she tried to look up, the girl's angry face was just a blur.

After the third grader ran out the door, Elizabeth came over and put her arm around Mary. "Don't pay any attention to her."

Audrey waggled her finger. "My grandmother has a name for people like that. NINCOMPOOP!"

Mary wiped her eyes with the bottom of her skirt while Audrey and Elizabeth laughed. Nothing seemed funny to Mary. She just wanted to go home.

4

Dad Is Puzzled

That night when Mary got home, she didn't feel like talking. Her father was at the kitchen table working on the daily crossword puzzle.

Her mother was replacing a door-knob.

"Hi, Mary. How was school?"

"Fine," Mary mumbled.

Mrs. Marony pointed her long screwdriver at the big glass jar on the counter. "Want a Mexican wedding cookie? I just made some today."

Mary nodded as she reached in the jar and bit into one. Mmmmm, she thought, confectionery sugar.

"How was the author?" her father asked.

"Okay."

"Did you get your book signed?"

Mary thought about her answer as she got herself some milk. If she said no, her father would ask why. If she said yes, she would be lying, and Mary never lied to her parents. "Mmmmmm ooomph," Mary said with her mouth full. "I left it in muh-my desk at school."

Sometimes Mary saved parts of the truth for later.

When her father changed the subject, Mary knew she was safe!

"What's a ten-letter word for fool? I've already tried numskull, dumbbell and ignoramus."

Mary and her mother laughed.

"Let's see," Mary said as she sat down next to her father and admired how handsome he looked in his crisp white shirt and his striped tie.

"Mmmmmm, how about Marvin?"

"Isn't that the boy in your class who bugs you?"

"Yes."

"Might just work. Let's see. Nope, Marvin has six letters."

Mary smiled. Her dad's sense of humor always brightened her day. He worked in real estate and sometimes when business was slow, he came home early.

"Hey, how 'bout DUNDERHEAD?" he asked. "That has ten letters."

Mary watched him pencil it in.

"Nope. It doesn't fit with the other words."

Mrs. Marony peeked inside the oven door to check on their dinner. "What about meathead?" she asked.

Mary shook her head as she watched her dad write the word in the margin of the newspaper. "Muh-meathead only has eight letters, Muh-mom."

When her father started to groan, Mary said, "Don't give up, Dad! We'll get it!" Then she ran to the bathroom. She had to go.

As soon as she got there, she remembered what Audrey had said in the *school* bathroom.

Two minutes later, Mary came flying back into the kitchen. "NINCOM-POOP!" she shouted.

"NINCOMPOOP?" her parents replied.

She and her mother leaned over her father's shoulder and watched him pencil the word in.

"IT FITS!" he yelled.

"I knew we'd get it, Dad," Mary said. "We're no fools!"

"Not us," he said as he put his arm around Mary and gave her a squeeze.

Mary had been home less than an hour, and already she felt much better.

5

The Spelling Wasp

The next morning after the children wrote in their notebooks, Mrs. Bird drew a yellow jacket on the board. "It's time for a spelling wasp," she announced.

"What's that?" Fred asked.

"It's a spelling bee, but I call it a spelling wasp because it's a lot tougher. In a regular spelling bee, the teacher chooses the words. In a spelling wasp, the class has to come up with the words."

"ALL RIGHT!" Marvin shouted as he reached for a dictionary.

"Just a minute, Marvin, you can't use any books. You have to know how to spell the words already."

"Oh," Marvin grumbled as he closed the book.

"What teams will there be?" Audrey asked.

"I thought we would have the west side of the room versus the east side. I have a surprise for the student who is left."

Everyone cheered. Mrs. Bird always gave books for prizes. Last time when they played grammar baseball, Fred Heinz won *101 Funny Jokes*.

"So," Mrs. Bird continued. "Get some scratch paper and write down a few words you know how to spell."

"What if you misspell one?" Audrey asked.

"I won't use it."

Mary smiled. She had her words already.

"I've got two no one can spell," Marvin bragged. "Tyrannosaurus rex and pharmacy."

And then he wrote them down:

"I've got three!" Fred said. And he wrote his down:

be youtiful
Halloween
Mississippi

Audrey was cautious. She only picked words she knew for sure were correct:

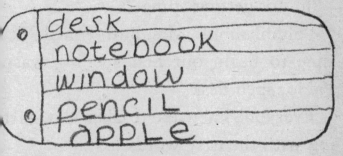

desk
notebook
window
pencil
apple

Mrs. Bird collected the scraps of paper and quickly crossed out the misspelled words. "Well, my list couldn't be more varied and unusual!"

Mary worried about pharmacy. She didn't know how to spell it.

"Okay, teams, line up on either side."

Audrey and Elizabeth were on the opposite team from Mary. They hoped she wouldn't get stuck on an *M* word. She seemed to be in a good mood again.

"If . . . you misspell a word," Mrs. Bird said, "I'll have to say 'Bzzzzzzzzzz!' And you sit down."

After the class laughed, Marvin said, "I'm not getting stung!"

"Shhh! Shhh!" Mrs. Bird replied. "It's time to begin our first spelling wasp. Pablo, spell desk."

Everyone knew the teacher was starting with the easy words first.

"D-e-s-k."

"Correct. Robert, spell it."

When the class laughed, Mrs. Bird snapped at them. "Shhh! Shhh!"

"I-t."

"Correct."

During the first round, all the children spelled their words correctly. Round two was different.

"Audrey, spell Mississippi."

Audrey fiddled with her necklace.

"Capital M, —i-s-s-i-s-s-i-p-p-i."

"Correct."

Mary gave her friend a silent cheer. She had spelled a tricky word.

"Fred, Tyrannosaurus rex."

When Fred couldn't spell it, Mrs. Bird said, "Bzzzzzzzzz."

Fred plopped in his chair. "I got stung by a dinosaur!"

Elizabeth was next. "Eh . . . , T . . . y . . . r . . . a . . . n . . . a . . . s . . . o . . . a . . . r . . . u . . . s."

Marvin was jumping up and down shaking his head.

"Bzzzzzzzz."

Elizabeth sat down.

When the next ten students got Bzzzzzed by Mrs. Bird, it was finally Marvin's turn. He was so excited. He got his own word!

"T-y-r-a-n-n-o-s-a-u-r-u-s r-e-x."

"Correct."

"I know all about dinosaurs," Marvin bragged.

By round three, there were just four people left, so Mrs. Bird had them all stand together. After they had correctly spelled words like Halloween, author, recess and island, Mrs. Bird said, "Audrey, your next word is . . . dumbbell."

The class laughed.

"It's a word in our dictionary," the teacher explained. "It can mean a weight that people lift to strengthen their muscles."

Mary shrugged. She just thought it meant fool. She kept her fingers crossed for her friend. Audrey was a good speller.

"D-u-m-b-e-l-l?"

"Bzzzzzzzzz!"

Audrey sat down.

"Pablo?"

Pablo giggled as he scratched his head. "Dumbbell? Eh, d-u-m-m-b-e-l-l."

"Bzzzzzzzzz!"

"Aaaugh!" Pablo groaned as he plopped in his chair.

"Mary, can you spell dumbbell?"

Mary smiled. Of course she could! "D-u-m-b-b-e-l-l."

"Correct! Now, Marvin," Mrs. Bird continued, "it's just you and Mary. Here comes the last and most difficult word."

Marvin was so excited he was springing up and down on his toes. He was sure it was his word, pharmacy.

"Nincompoop," Mrs. Bird said, trying to keep a straight face. "It's in the dictionary," Mrs. Bird explained. "It means fool."

Marvin stopped jumping. "Boy! That's a doozie. Well, I can spell poop. But, I'm not sure about the nincom."

When the class laughed, Mrs. Bird snapped, "Shhh! Shhh! It's time to be serious. Marvin, spell nincompoop."

Marvin tried, "N . . . i . . . n . . . c . . . o . . . m . . . e . . . p-o-o-p."

"Bzzzzzzzzz! Mary, if you can spell the word, you will be our spelling champ."

Mary smiled. She never stuttered when she spelled. Calmly, she turned and looked Marvin in the eye. "NIN-COMPOOP!" she said.

Oh, she thought, that felt so good!

"Aren't you going to spell it?" Mrs. Bird asked.

"Of course," Mary replied. "N-i-n-c-o-m-p-o-o-p."

Everyone looked at Mrs. Bird. Was she going to say, Bzzzzzzz?

She didn't!

"That's it, Mary! You're our champ!"

All the girls gathered around Mary and cheered.

Mary beamed. She couldn't wait to tell her dad.

"Lucky you!" Audrey said. "Now you get a prize."

Mary shrugged. She felt like she had already gotten her reward. She had called Marvin a nincompoop in front of the class and gotten away with it!

"Well," the teacher replied. "I think you will all agree that this is the best surprise I'll give this year."

The class looked at the teacher. She wasn't holding a book.

"What is it?" everyone asked.

"Mary has just won an invitation to have lunch today with the author Jan Berry!"

Everyone clapped and cheered—until they noticed Mary's reaction.

She wasn't clapping.

She wasn't cheering.

Mary looked like she was about to cry.

How could she face that author again after what happened yesterday? She couldn't go. She WOULDN'T go. Mary Marony ran out of the room!

6

The Hideout

When Mary didn't come back to the room, Mrs. Bird asked Audrey and Elizabeth if they knew where she had gone.

Audrey spoke first. "She has a special hideout in our school." Then she stopped. She wondered if she should tattle on her friend.

"It's the bathroom, behind the door," Elizabeth said. She knew this was important.

"Do you want us to go get her?"

Mrs. Bird shook her head. "No, you two girls go back to your seats. I have someone else in mind."

Mr. Fries! Audrey thought. Poor Mary! Now she would be blasted out of the bathroom with a foghorn!

As Mary hid behind the bathroom door, she began to worry. She had never run out of class before. She knew she shouldn't have. But she did.

Suddenly someone walked into the bathroom. "Mary?" the voice called.

Mary took a quick peek. It was Miss Lawton, her speech therapist!

Mary came out from behind the door and ran into her arms. "I'm s-so sorry! Am I in t-t-trouble?" she sobbed.

Miss Lawton's five bracelets jingled as she patted her on the back. "No, Mary, you're not in trouble. Your teacher, Mrs. Bird, sent me. She said we could go to my room and talk for a while. Would you like that?"

Mary nodded. Then she clung to Miss Lawton's dress as they left the bathroom and walked down the school hall.

Mary felt better when she got to her speech therapist's room. It was bright and cheerful. She looked at the shelves of puzzles, games and animal puppets as she wiped her eyes with her knobby green sweater.

Miss Lawton spoke slowly and clearly. "Sit down, Mary. Do you want to tell me what's bothering you?"

Mary took a deep breath. She felt comfortable and safe now. "Mrs. Bird said . . . I have to . . . have lunch with J-Jan Berry."

"That sounds like fun. I know she's your favorite author. We've talked about her books."

"She *is* my fav-favorite author, but . . ."

"But what?"

Slowly, Mary told her speech therapist the whole story about how she had stuttered in front of the school, and how the author would think she was dumb.

"Mary! That's not true. I met Jan Berry yesterday. She's a kind person, like you."

"You don't think . . . that Jan Berry . . . will think . . . I'm . . . dumb?"

"No," Miss Lawton replied. Then she added, "Mary, you are speaking so well."

"I am?"

"You are."

"But . . . what . . . if I . . . I st-stutter on a word?"

"Stop, take another breath and begin again."

"Even on *M* words?"

Miss Lawton reached for the monkey puppet, slid it on her hand and made the mouth open and close. "Let's practice a few *M* words. You'll see how well you can say them."

Mary picked up the hairy grizzly bear. "I'm ready."

And she did exactly what Miss Lawton did. Each time she came to an *M* sound and closed the monkey's mouth, Mary did the same thing to her puppet.

"Mmmmmmmmm."

"Mmmmmmmmm."

"Mmmmmary mmmmakes . . ."

"Mmmmmary mmmmakes . . ."

"Mmmmm Mary . . . makes . . . macaroni."

"Mmmmm Mary . . . makes . . . macaroni."

"See? You're terrific!" Miss Lawton exclaimed.

Mary gave her speech therapist a hug. She *felt* terrific.

"So, you'll have lunch with Jan Berry?"

"Yes!"

"Good. Now, what would you like to talk about?"

Mary worked the bear's mouth again. "Do you know . . . a ten-letter word . . . for fool?"

Miss Lawton made her puppet say another *M* sound. "Hmmmmmmm. I'll have to give that some thought. . . ."

7

Lunch with the Author

When Mary returned to the classroom, she went right up to the teacher.

"I'm . . . very sorry, Mrs. Bird. I won't run . . . out of the class . . . again."

"I know you won't, Mary. Now go and enjoy your lunch with Jan Berry. It's almost time."

Mary looked up at the clock. It was 12:25. "Th-thanks, Mrs. Bird."

Just as Mary was leaving the room, Elizabeth rushed over to her. "Mary! Don't forget your book. You have to get it autographed. This is your last chance."

"Oh, thanks, Liz!"

Audrey took off her necklace. "Here, you can wear this."

Mary studied the eight empty wooden spools of thread that were painted and strung on a green ribbon. "Gee, thanks, Audrey. I love the little purple and yellow flowers. You're such a good artist."

"Thanks. They're supposed to be morning glories. Whenever you get worried, just fiddle with them. They help me."

After Mary put the necklace on, she made a quick huddle with the girls, and jumped up and down.

"You two are the best friends I'll ever have." Then she broke away and hurried down the long hall to the open doorway of the library.

There she was.

Jan Berry.

Mary didn't notice the posters her library class had made, the computer printout that spelled the author's name

or the girl seated next to Jan Berry.
Mary just noticed the author's big smile
and messy hair.

The librarian greeted her right away.
"Mary! Come and sit here next to Jan
Berry."

"Thank you, Mr. Woods."

"Jan, this is . . ."

"Mary Marony. I remember she had my new book. Hi, Mary."

Mary shook the author's hand. What a memory! she thought as she sat down at the table.

Then the librarian introduced Mary to the other girl sitting next to the author. "This is Kitty Allen. She's in third grade."

Mary suddenly froze. It was her! *That* girl in the bathroom. "Huh-huh-hi," she stuttered.

Kitty didn't smile back. She just said a short, hi.

Why did *she* have to be here! Mary thought. Now she would stutter for sure with *her* around. Mary quietly set her book on the floor next to her feet. She would ask for the author's autograph later, when Kitty wasn't around.

By 12:35 P.M., the rest of the children had arrived and were seated around the two long library tables that were pushed together and decorated with woven place mats and miniature book covers. Mr. Woods and two mothers from the PTA were serving slices of double cheese pizza, tossed salad, and pouring juice.

Jan Berry looked at the fifteen silent children who were staring at her. "How about if each one of you tell me something about yourself? Your writing? Whatever you'd like to ask me. Mary, shall we start with you?" the author asked.

Mary shook her head. She wasn't ready. The author casually turned. "Kitty, why don't you start, then?"

Kitty put her pizza down. "Well, Mom calls me Kitty because I've been nuts about cats ever since I was a baby. My favorite book is *Cat on Vacation*. I've read it to James three times."

"James is your younger brother?"

"No, he's my cat."

Everyone laughed but Mary.

"I write in my diary every night like you do, *but,* ever since my brother sneaked into my room and read a few pages, I've kept it under lock and key. I like my privacy."

When Kitty glared at Mary, Mary knew what she was thinking. There's that second-grade spy!

"That diary key sounds like a good idea," Jan Berry said. Then she added, "I'm nuts about cats, too. I have four. Tux, Zeeb, Flower and Giz."

"Hey!" Kitty exclaimed. "Tux was the name of the cat in your book! Does your cat try to answer the phone when it rings?"

The author nodded. "That's Tux!"

This time Mary laughed. She could just picture the author's cat standing tall on two hind legs, clawing at the phone cord.

For the next twenty minutes, the children took turns talking about themselves and their writing and asking the author questions. When the conversation finally came around to the boy who was sitting next to Mary, Mary's knees started knocking. She *knew* she was next.

8

Discoveries

Mary fiddled with the spools of thread around her neck. Audrey said they had helped her.

"My name is Muh-muh-muh . . ."

When Mary got stuck on the *M* word, this time she remembered what Miss Lawton had told her.

Stop talking.

Take a breath.

And begin again.

"Mmmmmmary Mmmmarony. I'm
the one who st-st-stood up at the as-
semmmbly yesterday. Talking is hard
. . . for me sometimes. I even h-hid in the
bathroom be-because I felt bad about
st-stuttering in front of the whole sch-
school." Mary paused, and then talked
more slowly. "But, now I . . . don't have
to hide . . . anymmmmore. Miss Lawton
is . . . helping me . . . talk better."

When Mary finished, she noticed no one was laughing and Kitty had stopped making faces.

"I hid in the bathroom once too," Jan Berry said.

"*You* did?" Mary was surprised that a famous author like Jan Berry would do something dumb like that.

"I was the tallest person in my sixth-grade gym class and we were having dancing. It was a boys' choice, and when I was the only girl left without a partner, I ran to the bathroom and stayed there the rest of the gym period."

After Jan Berry twirled some hair around her fingers, she continued, "So Mary, what have you written about lately?"

"Mmmm-my family. The name of the st-story . . . I wrote this mmmmorning

. . . in my notebook was 'Sundays, Dad and I Sit on a House.' "

When everyone laughed, Mary did too. This was the *first* time she actually enjoyed talking in front of a group. And it was the first time she thought it was *fun* to make people laugh. She couldn't wait to tell Miss Lawton.

"Mmmm-my dad is in real estate . . . and sometimes he takes . . . mmm-me with him when he h-holds a house open. He calls that . . . sitting on a house."

Jan Berry smiled. "I'm so glad you're writing about your experiences. They make the best stories!" She looked around the group. "Especially the *little things* like Kitty reading to her cat, John noticing how the blinds jiggle when his dad snores, Sue's messy desk and

Mary's sitting on a house. Bravo!"

When the author finally stopped twisting her hair, Kitty said, *"You* should write a story about a character who puts knots in her hair."

Jan Berry laughed loudly. "True!" Then she stood up. "Well, I think you're a neat group of boys and girls. We shared a lot today."

As she walked to the door, the mothers handed her the posters and rolled-up computer printout. Mr. Woods shook her hand and thanked her for coming.

Then she waved to the boys and girls. "Thank you for the signs, the beautiful posters and the *great* conversation. Don't ever stop writing. I want to check *your* books out of the library in a few years."

Books!

Mary scooped hers off the floor and ran to the doorway. She *had* to get it autographed.

"WAIT!" she called. "W-would you sign this, please?"

Jan Berry put her things down in the hallway. "I'd love to. You spell your name M-a-r-y?"

Mary nodded. Then, as the author opened up her big purse, Mary said what she could never say at the assembly. "I . . . I *loved* your book very mmmmmmm-much."

"You did? Oh, I'm so glad, Mary. It took me a long time to write. However, finding a pen might take longer."

Mary smiled as she watched Jan Berry rummage in her purse.

"You would think I have lots of pens, Mary, but I'm always leaving them everywhere. Aha!" Finally she pulled out a green one that said JOE'S GARAGE.

Mary watched her write her autograph. She was secretly pleased it took so long.

"There," she said, handing Mary the book.

"Thank you!" Mary replied.

Jan Berry waved as she walked down the long hallway carrying all her stuff.

Mary waved back. She felt like she was saying goodbye to a new friend.

When she turned, Kitty Allen was standing in the doorway.

"Mary, can I talk to you?" Kitty hesitated. "I . . . I'm so sorry I was mean yesterday. I thought you were spying on me like my brother, and I just got *so* angry. I didn't know you saw Miss Lawton. I saw her in kindergarten and first grade."

"You did?"

"Yes. I couldn't say my *R* words. If I tried to say, the rabbit ran down the road, it came out, the wabbit wan down the woad. Every time someone asked me what I liked to do best in school, I'd say weading. I hated *R* words."

"I hate *M* words."

Both girls rolled their eyes.

"Well," Mary said. "I'm sorry too. Muh-my friends and I . . . *were* eavesdropping. And th-that . . . wasn't right. I know that now."

Kitty looked at Mary and smiled for the first time.

Mary smiled back.

"Want to see what Jan Berry wrote?" Mary asked as she flipped to the title page.

"Yes!"

And they read it together.

OTHER BOOKS
BY
JAN BERRY

Cat on Vacation
The Cat Who Liked Ice Tea
Grandfather's Secret
Queen of the Lost and Found

GHOST IN THE CLOCK
by
JAN BERRY

♡

Mary,
It was so nice to have pizza together and talk. Who would have guessed we had the same hide outs! (I'm glad we don't have to use them anymore.) Keep writing and laughing!

♡ Jan Berry